Working with Metal

Heather Hammonds

Photographs by Lindsay Edwards

Contents

NELSON

™

THOMSON LEARNING

Australia · Canada · Mexico · Singapore · Spain · United Kingdom · United States

The Blacksmith

Blacksmiths work with metal.
They make many different things.

They hammer,

bend,

and twist hot metal into many different shapes.

Blacksmiths must be careful
when working
with hot metal.

They need to wear
clothes that **protect** them.

A blacksmith wears:
- safety goggles
- thick gloves
- an apron
- boots

safety goggles

thick gloves

an apron

boots

The Forge

Blacksmiths heat metal in a **forge**.
A forge is like a fireplace.

coal

Coal is used to make the fire in the forge.
The fire needs to be very hot!

The Tools

Blacksmiths have many tools.
They use:

- **hammers**
  to hit
  the metal

- **tongs**
  to hold
  the metal

- **files**
  to shape
  the metal

- tools
  to punch
  holes in
  the metal

Blacksmiths also use an **anvil.**

An anvil is a tool, too.
It is a heavy block
of metal with a flat top.

Blacksmiths hit and bend
hot metal on the anvil.

anvil

Hot Metal

This blacksmith puts some metal in the forge. He wears gloves to hold the metal.

He waits for the metal to heat up.
Soon it turns dark red. The metal is now hot.
It is so hot that it is soft!

When the metal is hot,
the blacksmith takes it
out of the fire.
He puts it on the anvil.
He hits the metal
with a hammer.

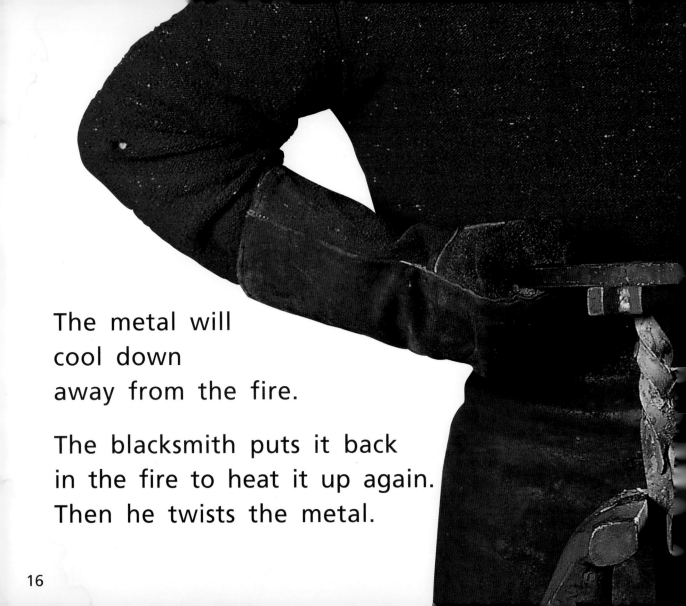

The metal will
cool down
away from the fire.

The blacksmith puts it back
in the fire to heat it up again.
Then he twists the metal.

16

The blacksmith
heats more metal.
He is making
a candlestick!

a metal
candlestick

17

Blacksmiths Long Ago

Long ago, there was a blacksmith's shop in most towns and villages.

Blacksmiths used metal to make and mend:

- wheels for wagons

- shoes for horses

- farm tools

- and many other things.

Blacksmiths Today

Some blacksmiths
still have
their own shops.

They hammer,
bend and twist
hot metal
to make things.

21

Metal Factories

Today, most metal things
are made in factories.

Machines can heat,
hammer and shape metal
much faster
than a person can.

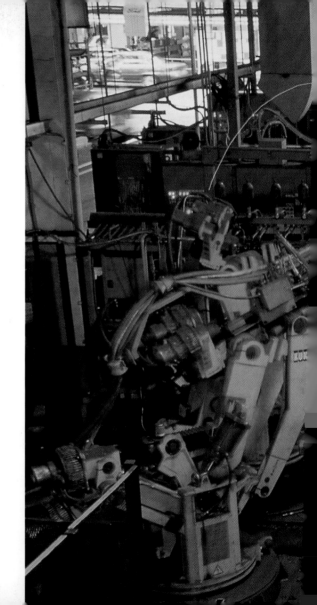

Glossary

anvil a heavy block of metal with a flat top

coal a brown or black rock

files tools used to shape and smooth metal

forge a place where metal is heated

hammers tools used to hit metal

protect to look after, take care of

tongs tools used for picking up and holding things

Index